SADDLEBACK
PUBLISHING·INC.

Barclay
Family
Adventures

Mountain Blizzard

BY

Ed Hanson

THE BARCLAY FAMILY ADVENTURES

Development and Production: Laurel Associates, Inc.
Cover and Interior Art: Black Eagle Productions

SADDLEBACK
PUBLISHING·INC.
Three Watson
Irvine, CA 92618-2767

Website: www.sdlback.com

ISBN 1-56254-556-6

Printed in the United States of America
08 07 06 05 04   9 8 7 6 5 4 3 2 1

CONTENTS

MEET THE BARCLAYS

Paul Barclay
A fun-loving father of three who takes his kids on his travels whenever he can.

Ann Barclay
The devoted mother who manages the homefront during Paul's many absences as an on-site construction engineer.

Jim Barclay
The eldest child, Jim is a talented athlete with his eye on a football scholarship at a major college.

Aaron Barclay
Three years younger than Jim, he's inquisitive, daring, and an absolute whiz in science class.

Pam Barclay
Adopted from Korea as a baby, Pam is a spunky middle-schooler who more than holds her own with her lively older brothers.

CHAPTER 1

The Surprise Trip

The Barclay kids loved the airport. All their favorite fast-food restaurants were there. There'd been no time to eat dinner at home, and they were hungry.

The telephone call for Paul Barclay had come just an hour ago. He and the kids' mother, Ann, were divorced. But just yesterday, Paul had come for a friendly visit.

Hanging up the phone, Paul said, "Ann, let's talk alone for a minute."

"I really hate it when they do that," said Aaron, who was 13.

Ann and Paul came back in the room.

"My company has a big construction project in Utah," Paul said. "Tomorrow morning I have to meet someone there. Why don't you kids come along? After my meeting, we could go skiing for a few days. Since it's school vacation, your mom has agreed."

Right away, nine-year-old Pam started asking a thousand questions.

"Later, Buttons," Paul said. "Right now, I have to call the airlines."

Luckily, there were four seats left on the last flight out. The problem was that the plane would leave in an hour.

"Okay, kids," Paul said. "We have to really, really hurry here!"

They had only 15 minutes before the cab would arrive to take them to the airport. Aaron and Pam started madly throwing things into suitcases. Their older brother, Jim, packed his duffel bag calmly. He was 17 now and would be a high school senior next fall.

Their mother was urging them to take warm clothes. Aaron looked at the red wool scarf she'd just put in his suitcase.

"Come on, Mom! We're not going to the North Pole!" he complained.

"Mom, no! Don't pack that ugly hat!" Pam shrieked.

Their mother just kept packing. Finally, she stuffed some long underwear into Pam's suitcase.

Paul was staring at the bulging bags.

"Good grief! We're only going away for a few days," he cried.

Just then, the taxicab pulled up and honked.

"Here, Aaron. I packed you guys some food for the plane," Ann said.

She handed him a large paper bag.

"Ann, I wish you could come along with us," Paul said.

Then he and the kids raced out the door and jumped into the cab. Ann looked out the window. She watched the cab drive down the street and then turn out of sight. Her face looked a little sad.

CHAPTER 2

Starting Out

Now the Barclays were eating fast food at the airport.

"It's a good thing Mom isn't here," Jim said. "She'd make us eat vegetables."

Paul winked at him. "The only vegetable in this airport is the pickle next to your sandwich," he said. He was happily eating a jumbo burger.

Then he thought for a moment. "I wish your mother were here," he said. He didn't seem to like being divorced.

Aaron had ordered too much food. He stuffed his leftover fries into his backpack.

"Oh, *gross*!" Pam cried.

"They taste good cold," said Aaron, "as long as you add ketchup."

"*Worse* than gross!" Jim added.

On the plane, the kids ate their snacks, but Paul wasn't hungry. He gave his pretzels and peanuts to Pam. She tucked them into her backpack.

The kids had lots of questions about the trip.

"First, we'll go to Salt Lake City, Utah," Paul explained. "Then we'll drive to the Grand Teton Mountains in Wyoming. We'll ski near a place called Jackson Hole."

"How high are the Grand Tetons?" Pam asked.

"Imagine a ranch house," said Paul. "You'd need to stack about 500 ranch houses on top of each other to reach the peak of Grand Teton."

Pam's eyes were wide.

"But, Dad," she asked, "why would you want to do that?"

Then Aaron had a question. "Are there any dangerous animals around there—grizzly bears, for example?"

"No grizzly bears," Paul said. "Grizzlies live around Yellowstone Park."

"But there *is* one very dangerous animal in the Tetons—the mountain lion," Paul went on. "If a mountain lion attacks, forget it! They have huge feet with curved claws and a mouthful of nasty teeth. And mountain lions are very strong—especially their legs and jaws. But, luckily, they rarely attack people."

A while later they could feel the plane begin to turn and descend. It flew over Great Salt Lake in Utah before landing in Salt Lake City. They were very tired after the long flight.

Paul picked up a rental car and drove to a motel. They all fell asleep as soon as their heads hit their pillows.

Paul got up early the next morning and called Ann. He talked quietly so he wouldn't wake up the kids. After reporting that they'd arrived safely, he promised to call her again when they got to the ski lodge.

Paul's business meeting lasted only two hours. When he returned to the motel, the kids were eager to get going. Paul looked at his map.

"Look at this," he said, pointing to a spot on the map. "We'll head north and drive into western Wyoming. Pretty soon after that we'll be in Jackson Hole. We should be skiing by this afternoon."

It took the Barclays only a few minutes to pack their bags in the trunk. Then they were on the expressway, heading north.

The kids had often gone skiing with their mother. They were all good skiers, but Jim was the best. Lifting weights to gain strength for football had helped his skiing a lot.

An expert downhill skier, Jim was also currently learning telemarking. His parents had given him telemarking skis for his birthday. Jim couldn't wait to try them in Wyoming.

CHAPTER 3

Grand Teton Valley

It was a beautiful day. As they drove through the valley, the kids were thrilled when they first saw the Grand Tetons in the distance. High above, the sun glistened off rock and snow thousands of feet up. Against the bright blue sky, a few little clouds sailed by the peaks.

Pam noticed all the sharp points of solid rock. She looked worried. "Is *that* where we are going to ski?"

Paul laughed. "Don't worry, Buttons. The ski slopes are nowhere near the tops of the mountains."

The nearer they got, the mountains looked bigger and bigger.

"There are coyote, moose, black bears, and deer in the Tetons," Paul said. "We may see some of them, if we're lucky. Not the black bears, though. Bears go to sleep for the winter.

"We'll probably also see some herds of elk. Elk are something like large deer. Every year, they come to spend the winter in the Tetons. They probably make good snacks for the mountain lions."

Then suddenly, Paul stopped the car and pointed.

"Look over there! *Moose!*"

They saw three tall animals. Their legs were very long, and their heads seemed too large for their bodies. Pam thought their large horns looked like trees growing out of their heads!

"*Weird!*" Aaron commented.

Then, just as Paul had predicted, they also saw a herd of elk. These animals were much better looking than the moose. There were dozens of them in the herd. Each one was snuffling the snow, looking for bits of grass to eat.

The land began to rise. Before long, the

valley was far below them. Looking down, they could see the Snake River winding along a meadow. Hundreds of spruce and cottonwood trees lined its banks.

As they climbed higher and higher, the sky started to look cloudy. After a while, they even saw some snowflakes.

"I hope it doesn't snow too much to ski," Jim said.

"Don't worry," Paul said. "I checked the weather. The forecast said it's supposed to be sunny for the next few days."

Now a beautiful lake lay just below them. The water was greenish blue, and it looked very clear.

"Can you believe it, kids? That lake was made by a glacier," Paul said.

"What's a glacier?" Pam asked.

"Thousands of years ago, the world became very cold," Aaron piped up. As a first-rate science student, he always seemed to know these things. "A big layer of ice covered a lot of the Earth back then."

"What happened to it?" Pam asked.

"The Earth gradually warmed up and it all melted," Aaron said.

"Could it happen again?" Pam asked.

"Maybe thousands of years from now. Not in our lifetime," Paul said.

The snowflakes became thicker as they drove on.

"Are you sure the weather is supposed to be sunny?" Jim asked.

"That was the report," said Paul. "Okay, Jimbo—see if you can get a weather update on the radio."

CHAPTER 4

Spin-Out

As Jim was looking for a weather station, Pam looked out the window.

"Look!" she said. "The sun is gone. The sky is all cloudy and gray now."

"Yeah, it already seems to be getting dark," Aaron chimed in.

Just then, the light snowfall became heavier. Before they knew it, there must have been an inch of snow on the ground! Paul had to slow down so the car wouldn't skid on the snowy road.

Soon there were *two* inches of snow on the ground! The car was struggling to get up the hills. And the snow was so dense they could hardly see at all.

Then Jim found a weather report. The voice on the radio said, "A sudden snow storm is moving in fast. State police have asked everyone to stay off the roads. Repeat: *This is a serious storm.*"

"I'm going to turn around," Paul said. "We'll go back to Jackson Hole for the night. We can ski tomorrow."

The kids were disappointed, but they knew their father was right.

Paul had trouble finding a place to turn around. He hadn't noticed that the road had become so narrow and steep.

"That's strange," Paul said. "We *were* on a main road. Did I turn onto a side road by mistake? Maybe I took the wrong fork back there."

Finally, Paul found a place to turn the car around. Now he was driving downhill very, very slowly. From time to time, the car skidded from side to side.

"I sure wish we had four-wheel drive," he said. His voice sounded nervous.

They crept along until they came to an especially steep part of the road.

"I remember this place," Jim said. "The

road goes along a high cliff where we looked down at the lake."

Suddenly, the snow was blinding. Now they couldn't even tell where the road was. Now Jim wished he hadn't mentioned the cliff—and so did everyone else!

"I'm going to have to stop the car," Paul said. "There's no choice."

He put on the brakes very carefully, but nothing happened. The hill was so steep that the brakes were useless in the slippery snow!

Picking up speed, the car went faster and faster. Suddenly, the wheels locked in a spinning skid! The car was out of control. They were all thrown backward, then forward and sideways. Paul struggled with the steering wheel, but it was hopeless!

They couldn't see anything but white, and now they had no idea where the cliff was. After sliding for several yards, the car hit something and stopped. Pam and Aaron screamed. Everyone in the car was thrown forward violently.

Pam and Aaron were still safely belted in the back seat. But the front door on Jim's side had been forced open. He was hanging partway out of the car. If he hadn't been wearing his seat belt, he, too, would have been thrown out.

Everyone was silent for a minute. No one knew exactly what had happened. But they were all grateful that they hadn't fallen over the cliff!

"Are you guys okay?" Paul asked in a weak voice.

The kids felt shaky, but they weren't really hurt. They could see the relief in their father's face when they told him they were safe and sound.

Then Pam began to sob and couldn't stop. Her little body was shaking hard. Aaron put his arms around her, and Jim reached back and patted her head.

Aaron tried to comfort her. "It's okay," he said. "We're not really hurt, Pam."

"I wish Mom was here," Pam sobbed.

"We'll all take care of each other," Jim said. "You don't need to worry."

The boys went on talking to Pam until they realized that their father hadn't said a word.

They looked at Paul. "Are *you* okay, Dad?" they both asked at once.

After a moment, Paul said, "Not really. My right leg is jammed against the wheel base." Then his voice trailed off and he let out a pitiful groan.

"I'm afraid my ankle is broken, kids. It hurts a lot—but I'll be okay once we get some help.

"I can help you kids figure out what to do—but I can't do anything myself. I won't be able to walk. The three of you will have to get us out of this mess. What do you say, guys? Do you think you can do it?"

CHAPTER 5

Saving Dad

Pam immediately stopped crying. Now the kids' biggest worry was their dad. They looked at him closely and noticed that he was pale and sweating. His body was all bent over in the driver's seat.

They could see nothing but swirls of white out the car windows. The ferocious wind was shaking the car from side to side.

"What should we do?" Pam whimpered. She had never been so frightened.

"I know what to do, honey," Paul said. "The problem is that we don't have what we need to do it."

Jim looked closely at his dad. "The first thing we need is to put you in the back seat, Dad. Then you can lie down."

"That's right," said Paul. "But you can't

move me until I have a splint on my ankle. On the other hand—if I don't lie down, I'm afraid I'll pass out. Did anyone bring anything that we could use as a makeshift splint?"

"Gosh, all I brought are my yo-yo and a package of fake worms," Aaron said. "Other than that, I just have the book I'm reading for my English class and the clothes Mom packed."

It was starting to get colder inside the car now. They could see frost forming on the windows.

"What did you bring with you, Jim?" Paul asked weakly.

"I brought a couple of paperback books and a football magazine. And, of course, I have my ski things and the clothes Mom packed."

"I really don't know what to do, then," Paul groaned.

"Well, how about me?" Pam said. "I brought my stuffed bear. I also brought along some books of puzzles, a handful of pencils, and my jump rope."

"Nothing there," said Paul. He was looking worse and worse.

"Wait a minute!" Aaron cried out. "It's *obvious!* What a dodo you are!"

"This is no time to bicker," Paul said.

"But Dad! I called *myself* a dodo!"

Now Aaron knew for sure that their dad was not in good shape.

"My idea," Aaron went on, "is to use my English book. It has thick covers."

"Excellent!" Paul said.

Forcing the car doors open, the boys jumped out to get Aaron's suitcase.

"Wait!" Paul cried. "Remember that we're near the top of the cliff!"

Jim and Aaron slowed down and carefully made their way to the trunk. They stayed very near the car. The wind and snow had become so strong that they could hardly stand. It was hard to hold on to the shaking car. In only a minute, they were covered with snow that stung their cheeks and eyes. But somehow they got the suitcase out of the trunk. They brought it inside the car.

"We need something to bind up my ankle," Paul said. "Pam, your jump rope might work. Jimbo—I hope you brought your Swiss army knife. We need something to cut the rope."

"Don't worry," Jim said. "I have it."

Aaron and Jim fought their way back to the trunk of the car.

They found Pam's suitcase and decided to bring Jim's bag in, too. To let them in the car, Pam had to push the door from the inside while they pulled. Finally, they opened the door and struggled inside.

For a minute, Jim and Aaron rested to catch their breath. Now it was almost too dark to see inside the car.

Then they got to work. They tore off the book covers and gently placed a cover on each side of Paul's right ankle. Next, they tied the rope around the book covers. Now Paul's ankle was fixed in a stiff position.

"That feels better already," he said.

Their next job was more challenging. They had to get their father into the back seat without hurting him.

"You'll have to move me without opening the doors," said Paul. "The wind is too strong. If it blows a door off, we'll have no shelter."

The kids lowered the seat backs as far as possible. Then Pam held Paul's leg as carefully as she could while the two boys rolled him onto the back seat.

Paul let out a deep breath. "This is going to be much better," he sighed.

The kids were relieved that their dad's face didn't look as pale now.

CHAPTER 6

A Cold Night

The car was rocking back and forth in the howling wind.

The kids discussed what to do. They decided that Jim and Aaron should stay in front while Pam got in back with Dad. This gave everyone as much room as possible. Still, the car was crowded. And by now they were very, very cold.

"Let's turn the engine on for a while and use the heater," said Jim.

"I wish we could," Paul said. "The problem is that there's probably snow in the tailpipe. That could push poisonous gas from the engine into the car. We can't afford to take that chance."

"But I'm r-really c-cold," Pam said through her chattering teeth.

"Hey, let's see what Mom packed for warm clothes," Jim suggested.

The kids went through their suitcases. They pulled out all the scarves, hats, mittens, sweaters, and long underwear their mother had packed. Now, they didn't care how they looked.

"Do you think Mom knew this would happen?" Pam asked.

"No way," Aaron said. "She just likes us to be ready for emergencies."

Then Jim said, "I'm getting hungry."

All of them were hungry! They ate the soggy French fries Aaron had put in his backpack. Then they ate the snacks Dad had given to Pam on the plane. Their meal didn't amount to much.

After that, there was nothing to do but try to go to sleep. They had lots of warm clothes and were protected by the car. They weren't in any danger of freezing, *but they were terribly cold.*

No one had very much room. Pam was perched on the big bump in the middle of the back floor. Up front, Jim and Aaron tried to sleep sitting up. Everyone was thirsty, but they had no water.

Pam was frightened. "I wish Mom was here," she said again.

"I don't," Aaron said. "Then she'd be in as much trouble as we are."

"We feel the same way, Buttons," Paul said. "In our hearts, we wish she was here. In our heads, we're glad that she's not."

Soon, the Barclays fell asleep. Each one was wondering if the car would be buried in snow when they woke up. But mostly, they wondered how close their car was to the top of the cliff.

CHAPTER 7

Jim's Long Journey

Daylight brought them some welcome surprises. For one thing, the Barclays were relieved that the car wasn't completely buried in snow.

And they were thrilled to see the sun shining brightly. As the sun rose, they looked out on a wonderland of sparkling snow dotted with fir trees.

Now they could see that their car was at the bottom of a steep slope. A lofty peak loomed above them. Paul could see it from the back seat. He studied it uneasily.

The best thing was that they couldn't see a cliff anywhere. They were sure it was out there—but everything was so white, it was hard to tell where one landform ended and the next started.

Still and all, everything wasn't exactly *wonderful*. They knew how dangerous their situation was. Being stranded on a remote mountain road in the middle of winter was no joke. Especially when no one even knew they were missing.

Using Jim's ski helmet as a sort of shovel, Jim and Aaron dug out one side of the car. Since the snow was up to the windows, it was a lot of work. They didn't bother to dig out the driver's side, but they were finally able to clear the tailpipe.

Jim climbed into the driver's seat. "Here's hoping," he said. He turned the key in the ignition.

"Oh, please, *please* start!" Pam cried. "I am so c-cold."

Nothing happened, so Jim tried again. But the engine didn't make a sound—not even a cough or sputter.

"It's no use," Jim groaned aloud.

"Don't worry," Paul said. "Even though we can't use the heater, we won't actually freeze. We are going to stay chilly, though."

"Well," Jim said, "so much for that. Now on to our next problem. What do we do about finding something to eat?"

"I don't know what we can do about that, either," Paul admitted. "But that's okay. We can survive for days without food. It won't be fun—but we can do it."

"Oh, great!" Aaron grumbled. Then he remembered something.

"Wait a minute!" he shouted. "We *do* have food! I forgot that Mom gave me a bag of snacks for the plane!"

He quickly pulled everything out of his backpack. Finally, there it was on the bottom—a squished-looking paper bag.

Aaron tore it open. They were all so hungry they could hardly wait to see what was in it. It turned out to be five peanut butter sandwiches, four apples, and a package of cookies!

"For someone who's not here, Mom is sure doing a lot to help us," Jim said.

They'd all been thirsty to begin with. After eating the peanut butter, their thirst was even worse. Lack of water was, in fact, their most serious problem.

"We could eat snow," said Pam. "It will melt inside us and turn into water."

"It doesn't work that way," said Paul. "Eating snow will just make you thirstier."

"Could we drink the water from the car's radiator?" Aaron asked.

"That won't work, either," Jim said. "The radiator water has antifreeze in it. And that stuff is poisonous."

"If only we could start a fire, we could melt some snow and drink it," Pam said.

"We could use the Swiss army knife to cut small branches off fir trees," Aaron said. "I don't think they'd burn very well— but maybe it would be enough. Then we could get the fire going by using the car's cigarette lighter."

"Let's try it," Paul said. "We must have water."

Jim frowned. "But what can we use for a container?" he asked.

"I know!" Pam cried out. "Why don't

we use one of the hubcaps?"

Their ideas worked. Aaron cut some fir branches and piled them up beside the car. Then, after several tries, Jim was able to light a twig with the cigarette lighter. He used the burning twig to light the pile of branches. For kindling, he used some pages from Aaron's English book. By now, there wasn't much left of it.

"My teacher isn't going to like this," Aaron said with a smile.

They filled a hubcap with snow. When the snow melted, they passed it around so everyone could have a sip.

"Not bad," Paul said.

The small fire even gave the shivering Barclays a little bit of warmth. So far, they were managing to survive.

Sometimes my little brother and sister amaze me, Jim thought to himself.

CHAPTER 8

Overnight in the Mountains

Even though they were all more comfortable now, Paul and Jim were worried. How could they be rescued if no one knew they were there?

"You know, Dad," Jim said, "there's only one thing to do now."

"I know," Paul replied. "All night, I kept waking up and thinking about that. I don't see any other way. You're going to have to ski out and find help.

"But, Jimbo," he said, "I hate to have you take off alone. I'm afraid we could be 20 miles from the main road."

"I can do it, Dad. Don't worry!"

After months of weightlifting and

34

jogging, Jim was in excellent physical shape. He had his telemarking skis and the know-how to use them. If he had to, he was sure he could ski for 20 miles.

It was important for Jim to leave as soon as possible. At this time of year, darkness came early. He put on his fleece ski clothes, hat, and gloves. He was already wearing his insulated ski boots. Before Jim started off, Paul made him take extra mittens and wrap two wool scarves snugly around his neck.

"Come on, Dad! You're worse than Mom," Jim grumbled.

Since Jim would need the most energy, Paul gave him the rest of the peanut butter sandwiches. The apples had already been eaten. That left the others with nothing but a few cookies.

Aaron remembered the soda bottles he'd forgotten to throw away. They quickly filled the bottles with melted snow and gave them to Jim. He was finally ready. It was time for him to take off.

Jim bent over Paul and gave him a hug. He could see how worried his father was.

He also hugged Aaron and Pam. Then he turned and started toward the road—or at least what he *hoped* was the road. In the blanketing world of white, it was hard to make anything out clearly. Aaron and Pam watched him point his skis outward and start up the hill. The climb looked very difficult. Luckily, Jim was able to do it, although he moved slowly.

When he reached the top of the hill, Jim looked back and held up his thumbs.

Pam grinned and cheered. "That must mean he found the road," she said.

Then they watched him ski away. He looked smaller and smaller as he skied into the distance. Finally, he went over a rise and disappeared.

The wind kept blowing in Jim's face. Everything was white. When the road curved, it was difficult to see where it went. Jim made a lot of false starts. Each time, he had to make his way back. Then he'd try another direction until he found the road again. It was very tiring.

Jim wasn't the only living creature in the landscape that day. He saw eagles soaring in the sky and a large herd of elk not far away. From time to time, he also saw tracks in the snow—tracks as big as dinner plates. They belonged to an animal with enormous padded feet. He guessed it must be a mountain lion.

Jim clearly remembered what his dad had said in the car. "Mountain lions rarely attack humans." But he didn't say that mountain lions *never* attacked humans. Apparently, there were exceptions. Jim gulped. He knew that he'd be defenseless if he was attacked.

Jim stopped only once to drink some water and eat half a peanut butter sandwich. By mid-afternoon he was quite exhausted. He'd been skiing for hours— mostly with a strong wind hurling snow in his face.

The mountain peaks rose up high to

the west. Jim knew what that meant. The sun would set even sooner than usual. When it disappeared behind those mountains, the darkness would be complete. He had a pretty good idea that he'd be in the mountains overnight.

It had been around 20 degrees all day—not counting the wind-chill factor. It would be a whole lot colder at night. Knowing what he had to do, Jim was grateful that his telemarking lessons had included some survival training.

First, he had to find a fir tree that had sloughed off a pile of snow. This part was easy. He found one right away.

The next part, however, was very difficult—especially since he was so tired. He had to dig a tunnel underneath the pile of snow. This would make a sort of buried igloo. He knew it was his only chance to get through the coming night without freezing to death.

Jim used his skis as shovels. They were too narrow to work well, but he had no choice. He dug until he was so tired that he could hardly stand.

At last, he finished making the snow cave. All he had left to do was crawl in. He wiggled into it, feet first. Then he filled in the opening, leaving only a small hole so he'd have air to breathe. He knew that he still wouldn't be warm. Even with his body heat trapped in the snow cave, the temperature would still be in the 20s.

Jim worried about Dad and Aaron and Pam, who were depending on him. He was also nervous about the mountain lion tracks. What would he do if a lion got interested in him? It could easily paw its way into his snow cave. Now Jim realized that he'd probably have a sleepless night.

But he was wrong. He was so exhausted that his worries about his family and the mountain lion weren't enough to keep him awake.

Twice he woke up in the night. The first time, his right leg was cramped. As soon as he shifted position, he fell back asleep.

The second time he awoke, Jim thought he heard something. Was he imagining the distant roaring sound? But then the thundering roar became louder and louder.

The ground began to shake a little. Then it shook faster. Suddenly, the ground was shaking so hard Jim was afraid that his snow cave would collapse. But suddenly, the noise and the shaking stopped at the same time.

All was complete silence now. This time, though, Jim couldn't fall back to sleep. All night he lay awake listening.

CHAPTER 9

The Cliff Is Found

After Jim left, Aaron took his ski helmet and shoveled out the driver's side of the car.

"I'm going to tramp through the snow a ways and see what I can see," he told his dad and sister.

"Don't go too far," Paul said. "And please be careful, Aaron. We're still not sure how close we are to the cliff."

Pam watched Aaron slowly trudge off, half digging and half trampling his way. The snow was very deep. Then Aaron just disappeared. It happened so suddenly that it took Pam a moment to realize that he wasn't there.

She jumped out of the car and slowly went over to where she had last seen him.

She looked down and gasped.

It was the cliff! The valley was so far below that the trees looked like little dots!

A few feet down, Aaron was clinging desperately to a small tree on the cliff wall. The little tree was bent double with his weight. Aaron's feet were dangling in mid-air! Pam was so frightened that her knees felt weak.

"Pam! Help me!" Aaron moaned. "I can't hold on much longer!"

Pam could see that her brother's arms were shaking and the little tree's roots were starting to loosen.

Aaron wasn't far below her. If she reached down—and he reached an arm up—they could touch hands. The problem was that Pam was too small to haul Aaron up the cliff. She knew that if she tried it, his weight would drag her over the edge.

"Hold on, Aaron!" she cried out. "Don't give up! Please, don't give up! I'll be right back!"

When she told her father, Paul wasted

no time. He sat up and opened the car door. In a moment, he was dragging himself toward the cliff on his stomach. Pam was amazed at how fast he was moving. Soon both of them reached the cliff and looked down at Aaron.

Pam held her breath as her father leaned over and reached down. Because he was so much taller than Pam, he'd be able to get a firm grip on Aaron's arm.

"Aaron, keep looking up!" Paul cried out. "*Whatever you do, don't look down!* Hold onto your tree with one hand and grab my arm with the other."

When Aaron reached up, Paul gripped his arm tightly.

"Now, let go of the tree and grab my arm with your other hand," Paul said.

Then, for some reason, Aaron looked down! Suddenly, he froze in terror.

"I can't let go," he said in a voice that Paul could barely hear. As he spoke, the roots of the small tree pulled farther from the wall. The movement knocked a few big clumps of snow down the cliff.

"Aaron!" Paul cried. "You must let go! *The tree is coming loose!*"

Still frozen with fear, Aaron didn't let go of the tree.

"Close your eyes," Paul cried. "Take a deep breath."

Aaron closed his eyes and took in a big gulp of air. Then, he let go of the tree and grabbed his father's arm. Just as he did, the tree roots ripped out of the cliff and the little tree tumbled down to the valley.

Very slowly and carefully, Paul pulled Aaron up by inching backward on his stomach. When he thought it was safe, he grabbed Aaron around the waist and hauled him all the way up.

Pam clapped and cheered. While Paul hobbled toward the car, she hurried Aaron to the front seat. Then she piled as many clothes on him as she could find. *Keeping him warm will help him recover from his shock*, she said to herself.

After a while, Paul said, "Aaron, I'm

mighty proud of you for letting go of the tree. I can only imagine how terrifying that must have been."

Aaron's life-or-death experience had worn them all out. No one felt like talking. There wasn't much to do but sit in the car. The day seemed very long. As the hours dragged on and on, the Barclays had plenty to worry about.

CHAPTER 10

Stampede

The next morning, Jim lay still for a while, listening hard for any more noises. His muscles felt sore from his cold night in the cave. He was sure that the stiffness would go away once he got moving. The important thing was that he'd survived a night alone in the mountains.

Using both his hands and feet, Jim pushed away the snow in the front of his cave. Then he wriggled his way out.

The first thing he saw was the plate-sized tracks. They circled the cave opening a few times and then continued on. There was no sign that the animal had tried to dig its way in. Did this mean that the mountain lion wasn't interested in him? Or was the mountain lion still hiding somewhere, just biding its time until Jim came out?

Jim looked around cautiously before eating and drinking a little. Then he put on his skis and climbed up a rise leading back to the road.

He could see nothing but snow, mountains, blue sky, and trees. He sensed that something was different, though. There was something strange about the land. Everywhere else, the snow was smooth and rolling. Here, it looked messy. Even at a distance he could see that the snow had been disturbed. He could even see trees sticking up at strange angles.

Then he knew what the roaring sound during the night had been. An avalanche had been triggered by the huge snowfall!

Thousands of tons of snow and ice had come crashing down the mountain. All the trees, rocks, and dirt in its path had been carried along with it. Jim was worried. The avalanche could have buried the car and his family! Even worse, it could have swept them all down the side of the mountain!

Jim felt panicky. He wanted to turn around and go back to the car. But it would take him all day just to get there!

And then he'd have to make this trip again—but without food. Jim knew that he was the family's only hope of rescue. There was nothing to do but go on.

Jim didn't know whether he had one mile to go or ten. As he came over a high rise, he saw a dark patch of something not far away. Strangely, it seemed to be *moving*. And it was moving toward *him*!

Now he could see that it was a herd of elk. The animals were all running at full speed. They seemed to be in a panic. Jim remembered that his father had said that mountain lions sometimes ate elk for snacks. Could a lion be the cause of the stampede? This wasn't a good situation.

The herd of frantic elk was closer than he'd realized. And these animals were *big!* Each elk must have weighed at least 500 pounds. Jim stared at them. They were almost on top of him now and moving really fast.

To get out of their path, Jim started to roll down a slope. Now he could feel the ground beneath him shaking from the stampeding hooves!

Jim saw dozens of legs coming at him. He tried to roll faster, but they were almost on him! The noise was deafening. He covered his head with his arms as the elk thundered by. They missed him by only a few yards. Then they were gone.

CHAPTER 11

Avalanche!

Paul, Aaron, and Pam could hear the distant rumbling. It became a loud roar, and the ground began to shake violently.

"Avalanche!" Paul shouted.

Something hit the side of the car with an enormous thud. Then another object came crashing down through the roof! It looked like a jagged piece of rock.

As even more objects crashed down, Paul was afraid the car would tip over.

Then there was silence. The terrible noise and violent movement stopped as suddenly as it had started.

Aaron tried to look out the window, but all was blackness.

"Do you think we're buried, Dad?" he asked fearfully.

Pam peered out the window on her side of the car.

"It's so dark outside that I can't see anything but stars," she said.

"Stars!" Aaron cried. "If you can see stars, then we *aren't* buried!"

A large chunk of flying ice had hurtled through the windshield. Now the car could no longer trap their body heat. The Barclays could already feel the temperature drop as the cold air rushed in.

Gathering all the extra clothes they could find, the kids stuffed them into the gaping hole.

At dawn, Paul and the kids could hardly believe what they saw. On the passenger side of the car—not 30 feet away—were several toppled trees.

Behind them was a wall of snow about 10 times higher than the car! If the avalanche had been any closer, they would have been buried for sure!

They all swallowed hard.

Paul closed his eyes and sighed. He was

beginning to wonder how much longer they could go on. The last cookie had been eaten yesterday. Paul knew the kids had to be hungry. He was hungry himself. And now they'd nearly been buried alive! Was this going to be the end for him and his kids?

CHAPTER 12

Jim's Narrow Escape

Shaky and out of breath, Jim rested in the snow. He knew how close he'd been to getting trampled! Luckily, he still had his skis and poles. Everything seemed okay— but why did he have this weird feeling that he was being watched?

Then he saw it at the top of the rise. It was crouched only 20 feet away, staring down at him. He could see the quivering leg muscles and enormous, plate-sized feet. Its eyes were the color of honey.

Jim didn't have much time. He watched the lion's shoulders ripple as it growled and prepared to charge.

Somehow I have to make myself look as

large as possible. *It's my only chance!* he thought to himself.

Slowly—very slowly—Jim stood up. His eyes never left the mountain lion. He reached down and picked up his skis while keeping his eyes glued to the eyes of the beast.

Jim made no sudden movements. Then, holding a ski in each hand, he slowly extended his arms as far as he could away from his sides.

The cold, yellow eyes bored into him and flickered. All the muscles tensed. The lion snarled, showing enormous front teeth and a long, nasty looking tongue. Jim could hardly believe it when the mountain lion turned and casually loped off.

Jim let out his breath. He'd never know why the mountain lion backed off. But he *did* know that he couldn't wait for this adventure to end!

Now he had to get all the way back up the steep slope before he could be on his way again. By now, he was very, very tired.

He struggled up the hill, knowing there were many more miles to go before the day was out. And what if he had to spend another night in the mountains?

As he skied on, Jim resolved that he could do whatever he had to do. Before long, he heard a noise. It was the sound of running water! He thought it must be coming from underneath the snow.

Stopping, he carefully poked ahead with his ski poles. He knew how serious it would be if he fell into water. In bitter cold, there's nothing more dangerous than getting wet. The consequences were clear to him: With no way to dry himself, he'd surely freeze in a short time!

He took a few steps and poked the snow again. This time, the pole went right through the snowdrift. Now he could see the water! He went on this way, poking holes, until he was sure of the creek's path. Finally, he found the bridge that arched over the creek.

To make sure that he stayed on the

slippery, narrow bridge, Jim had to keep poking with his poles. He was in constant danger of falling off. But he was so exhausted, he almost didn't care.

At last, he made it over the bridge. By now, his legs felt weak and his arm muscles were so sore he couldn't move them without pain. He'd eaten the last of the peanut butter sandwiches a few hours ago. He wondered if he could go on.

CHAPTER 13

Surprise Guest

Numb with hunger, Aaron, Pam, and Paul were starting to feel a little strange.

"I'm worried about Jim," Aaron said.

"He'll be fine," Paul said, trying to be cheerful. "I'm sure he's just fine."

Dad doesn't sound right, Pam thought to herself. *He must be really worried.*

To stay calm, they started talking. They talked about the family. They wondered what Mom was doing. Dad told them about his latest construction project.

Aaron talked about his dream of becoming a scientist. Pam talked about a book she'd just read. They were all afraid to talk about Jim.

Once, Aaron thought he heard a humming sound—but it stopped before anyone else heard it. A few minutes went by. Then Pam spoke up.

"I hear something," she said. "I sure hope it's not another avalanche."

They all looked up. Nothing was moving on the peak above them. Then the humming noise started again. This time there was no mistaking it. It was the sound of engines. Aaron and Pam jumped out of the car and looked for a plane. But there was no plane in sight. Then they looked around the snowy landscape.

They yelled when they saw the four dots in the distance. The dots seemed to be coming in their direction! After a while, they could see that the moving dots were snowmobiles. One of the drivers waved!

"*Jim got through!*" Paul cried.

The snowmobiles came speeding up, sending snow flying in all directions. Jim jumped off the first snowmobile and ran toward Pam and Aaron.

"You're all right!" he cried out. "You weren't hit by the avalanche!" Then he saw the great wall of rubble and snow piled up beside the car.

He shuddered. "That was a close call, wasn't it? I heard the avalanche—but I had no way of knowing if it had hit you."

The driver of the other snowmobile was hurrying toward them. The figure was so bundled up that its face was hidden in hat and scarves. The next thing they knew, both Pam and Aaron were nearly being smothered with hugs. Then Pam recognized the familiar blue eyes peeking out between the scarves.

"*Mom?!*" she gasped.

"Mom, I don't believe it's you! How did you get here?" Aaron cried out.

"Dad didn't call from the ski lodge as he'd promised. That made me worry. I called the ski lodge and the police in Jackson Hole. No one knew anything, so I hopped on the first plane going out," Ann explained. "You guys can't imagine how relieved I was to see Jim walking into the police station."

"Oh, Mom! I've never been happier to see anyone!" Pam cried as she hugged her mother again.

Ann held out a large paper bag. Aaron was the first to notice the fast-food logo on the outside of the bag.

"*Food!*" Aaron cried. He ripped the bag open and sighed at the unmistakable smell of cheeseburgers.

Then Ann asked, "Where's your dad?"

"He's still in the car," Pam said. "He got hurt and he can't walk."

Ann ran over to the car. She opened the door and climbed into the back seat.

"Paul, you're hurt!" she cried out. She reached out and touched his face.

"I'll be fine," Paul assured her. "Oh, Ann, it's so good to see you!"

"Not as good as it is to see *you*! I felt so helpless, Paul! I couldn't bear knowing that you and the children were lost."

"You helped us more than you know," Paul said gratefully. "Without even being here, you fed us and kept us warm." He smiled at her and tried to sit up.

Then the kids saw something even more amazing than the avalanche. Mom and Dad were kissing! Pam and Aaron looked at each other. For a few seconds, they stopped eating their French fries.

By now, two more snowmobiles had reached them. The drivers got off and began to unstrap first aid equipment.

The trip back to Jackson Hole was exciting. The kids had never ridden on snowmobiles. The biggest treat of the day, however, was their *warm* motel room and its *hot* shower.

Paul was soon propped up in bed with his ankle in a genuine cast.

"Jimbo, tell us about your trip back to the road," he said.

"The wildlife almost did me in," Jim replied. Then he went on to tell them all about the elk and the mountain lion.

"Otherwise," he said, "I just got really tired. At one point, right after I crossed a bridge, I actually thought about giving up.

But I knew I couldn't do that. I had no choice but to get moving again. There was no food or water left, and I knew it would be dark in a few hours. The situation was pretty desperate.

"So, I just straightened up and looked ahead, hoping the road would be cleared. I honestly didn't have the strength for any more detours.

"In the distance, I saw a plowed road— *a plowed road with cars going by!* Can you imagine how I felt? When I realized what I was seeing, I knew that our ordeal was almost over."

A little later, Paul started to chuckle.

"Hey, you guys, I just thought of something! There are still a few days of school vacation left. Maybe you three kids can get in some skiing after all!"

"No, thanks," said Jim.

COMPREHENSION QUESTIONS

Who and Where?

1. In what city and state did the Barclays' plane land?

2. In what mountain range did the Barclays plan to ski?

3. Who thought of making a splint out of book covers?

4. Who almost got trampled by a herd of elk?

5. Who came close to falling down a cliff?

6. Whose ankle was broken?

7. Ann Barclay called the police in what city and state?

Remembering Details

1. What weather conditions caused the Barclays' auto accident?

2. What leftover food had Aaron stuffed into his backpack?

3. What container did the Barclays use to melt snow?

4. What natural phenomenon caused the ground to shake?

5. Who shared the back seat of the car with Paul?

6. After being rescued, how did the Barclays travel back to Jackson Hole?